Nate the Great
on the
Owl Express

Nate The Great
on the
Owl Express

by Marjorie Weinman Sharmat
and Mitchell Sharmat

illustrated by Martha Weston
in the style of Marc Simont

A YEARLING BOOK

SPECIAL GUEST APPEARANCES BY
Olivia Sharp, Willie the Chauffeur,
and Hoot the Owl
from the Olivia Sharp, Agent for Secrets series
by Marjorie and Mitchell Sharmat

Text copyright © 2003 by Marjorie Weinman Sharmat and Mitchell Sharmat
Cover art and interior illustrations copyright © 2003 by Martha Weston
New illustrations of Nate the Great, Sludge, Fang, Annie, Rosamond, and the Hexes by Martha Weston based upon the original drawings by Marc Simont
Extra Fun Activities text copyright © 2004 by Emily Costello
Extra Fun Activities illustrations copyright © 2004 by Jody Wheeler

All rights reserved. Published in the United States by Yearling, an imprint of Random House Children's Books, a division of Penguin Random House LLC, New York. Originally published in hardcover in the United States by Delacorte Press, an imprint of Random House Children's Books, New York, in 2003.

Yearling and the jumping horse design are registered trademarks of Penguin Random House LLC.

Visit us on the Web! randomhousekids.com
Educators and librarians, for a variety of teaching tools, visit us at RHTeachersLibrarians.com

Library of Congress Cataloging-in-Publication Data is available upon request.
ISBN 978-0-385-73078-5 (trade) — ISBN 978-0-385-90102-4 (lib. bdg.)
ISBN 978-0-440-41927-3 (pbk.) — ISBN 978-0-307-55847-3 (ebook)

Printed in the United States of America
28 27 26 25
First Yearling Edition 2004

*To each other
and our long journey together.*

—M.W.S.

*To Marjorie and Mitchell—
with thanks for the great pleasure of getting to come
along on these wonderful trips with Nate.*

—M.W.

CHAPTER ONE

Curvy Beak, Pointy Claws

I, Nate the Great, am a detective.
Right now I am a
clickety-clack
rocking-back-
and-forth
detective.
I am on a train.
My dog, Sludge, is with me.
He is a detective too.
We are on a case.
We are bodyguards.
For an owl.
Her name is Hoot.
She belongs to my cousin Olivia Sharp.

The case started this morning.
Sludge and I were visiting Olivia
in San Francisco.
Olivia is also a detective.
This morning she said,
"Hoot needs to take a train
to a special owl doctor
in Los Angeles."
"A plane is faster," I said.
"Hoot doesn't like to fly," she said.
"I, Nate the Great, say
that is a good enough reason
for an owl to see a doctor."
Olivia tossed her boa around her neck.
She always wears a boa.
"Glad you think so," she said.
Then she tossed her boa
around my neck,

looked me straight in the eye,
and said, "You'll take Hoot
on the train for me.
I know I can count on you."
Olivia pulled me over
to a covered birdcage.
She lifted the cover.

I looked into two huge staring eyes.
Then I saw a big head,
a curvy beak,
and sharp pointy claws.
"What big eyes she has!" I said.
"Yes, and she's easy to feed,"
Olivia said. "She eats mice."
"You have told me, Nate the Great,
more than I want to know."
But Olivia wasn't finished.

CHAPTER TWO

Wanted: A Bodyguard

"I will catch up with you later,"
Olivia said.

"How? Where? When?"

"When the time is right," she said.
"But for now, Willie will drive
the three of you in my limo
to the train station."

Willie is Olivia's chauffeur.
We had worked on another case
together. I knew him well.

"Anything else I should know?" I asked.

"Just one little thing," Olivia said.

"You'll be a bodyguard."

"What? Who am I guarding?"
"Hoot, of course."
"Hoot? Why does Hoot need a
bodyguard?"
Olivia handed me a piece of paper.
"Look at this," she said.
I, Nate the Great, read,

It will be
a happy day
when Hoot the
owl flies
away.
Your
neighbor

"Hmmm," I said. "Do you think
someone in this building
is trying to get rid of Hoot?"

"Yes, and I made sure
all the neighbors know that Hoot
will be on the train today.
So if the note writer takes the train
and tries to get at Hoot,
we'll catch him or her."
"Good plan," I said. "But why
aren't *you* Hoot's bodyguard?"
Olivia tossed her boa.
"Because my neighbors know
that I know
what they look like.
If they see me on the train,
I might scare them off.
That's why I need *you*!"
And that's how I, Nate the Great,
became a bodyguard
for an owl.

CHAPTER THREE

All Aboard

Sludge and I got into
the back of the limo.
Willie was already in the front seat
with the covered cage beside him.
I was glad it was not beside me.
Willie turned around.
"Miss Olivia wants Hoot
to get a good day's sleep," he said.
"So keep her cage covered."

"No problem," I said.
"But is an owl allowed on a train?
And a dog?"
"Miss Olivia took care of everything,"
Willie said.
"I believe it," I said.
Willie started the limo and we were off.

I took a pad of paper
and a pencil from my pocket.
I wrote a note to my mother.

Dear Mother,
I have a new case.
It is in a cage.
I hope to keep it
there. I will be back.
Love,
Nate the Great

When we got to the train station,
I handed the note to Willie.
"A note for your mother, Mr. Great?
I will send it to her."
"Thank you," I said.

On the train Willie carried the cage
down the aisle.
Sludge was sniffing.
People were staring at us.

At last Willie stopped at a door.
He opened it.
We went into a room.
Willie put the cage on a table,
patted Sludge, saluted, and left.
And there we were.
The three of us.
Hoot, Sludge, and me.

CHAPTER FOUR
Achoo!

The train pulled out of the station.
Sludge kept looking at the cage.
Was he trying to be a good bodyguard
or was he afraid of Hoot?
"I am going out to see
what I can learn," I said.
"Stay here and guard Hoot."
Sludge did not look happy.
I opened the door, walked out,
and closed the door behind me.
There was a room next to mine.
The door was open.
A man and a woman were inside.

"Hello," I said. "Do you know
an owl named Hoot?"
The man laughed. "Hoot who?"

I walked on.
Two boys were coming down the aisle.
"Do you know an owl
named Hoot?" I asked.
They laughed. "Hoot-toot-toot."

I walked on.
I saw another open door.
Inside, a lady was soaking her feet.
"Do you know an owl
named Hoot?" I asked.
"Yes. She lives in my building."
"I see," I said. "Is anyone else
from your building on this train?"

"Yes. Two men. One is a musician.
He's in the lounge. I don't know where
the other man is."
"Last question. Do you like Hoot?"
The lady scrunched up her face.
"She makes me sneeze.
Duck! I'm about to sneeze right now."
"Thank you for the information," I said.
"I will use it right now.
Especially the last part."
I ducked and rushed away.
I knew that lady had a reason
for not liking Hoot.

CHAPTER FIVE

The Look-alike

I walked on.
I passed rows of people.
They were sitting, talking,
reading, sleeping, or
just looking out the windows.
I found the lounge.
I saw a man with a guitar.
"My name is Nate the Great," I said.
"Tell me, do you like Hoot the owl?"

"Sure," he said. "She screeches.
And it's like music to my ears."
"Glad to hear that," I said.
"Now I'm looking for another man
who knows Hoot."
The musician smiled. "The Owl Man.
He looks like an owl.
He's sitting back there.
You'll know him when you see him."

"Thank you," I said.

"I'm writing a song about sounds,"
the musician said.

*"A wolf can howl without a towel
but sometimes needs to use a vowel."*

"Well, have a good time
trying to rhyme," I said.

"Hey, nice rhyme," the musician said.

I walked back to where
people were sitting in rows.

I stared at everyone.

Then I saw a man
wearing a spotted shirt
and big yellow glasses.

His hair stuck up in two points.

The Owl Man.

I bent over him.

"Perhaps you like Hoot the owl?" I asked.

"Perhaps I don't," he said.
"People keep telling me
I look like her big brother."

I walked on.
Hmmm. Maybe Hoot did need a bodyguard.
Three people who knew her
were on this train.
Two of those people might not like her.
I went back to my room.
I opened the door.

Sludge was standing there.

With his ears perked up.

Like a good bodyguard.

He wagged his tail.

I looked at Hoot's cage.

It was just where Willie had put it.

"Fine job, Sludge," I said.

Sludge wagged his tail again.

"Time to rest," I said.

I sat down on a couch.

I looked out the window.

I saw trees going by.

And mountains.

And lakes.

I closed my eyes.

CHAPTER SIX
The Cage

I heard a voice.
It belonged to my friend Annie.
She was talking in rhyme.
"Do you know where you are?
Take a big guess.
You're asleep on this case,
on the Owl Express."
What was Annie doing on this train?

Then I heard a strange voice.

It belonged to Rosamond.

She is the only strange person I know.

She was also talking in rhyme.

"Don't snooze. Find clues.

Try hard. Bodyguard."

I sat up suddenly.

I, Nate the Great, had been asleep.

Had I been working on the case
in my dreams?

Why did bad rhymes get into my dreams?

Perhaps I was trying to give myself a clue.

I looked at the cage.

Was Hoot still asleep?

Was she hungry? Was she happy?

I, Nate the Great,
hoped the answers were
yes, no, and yes.
I got up and walked to her cage.
Willie had told me to keep it covered.
He had told me to let Hoot sleep.
But, I, Nate the Great,
had a job to do.
I lifted the cover.
Hoot wasn't asleep or hungry or happy.
She was gone!

CHAPTER SEVEN

Pancake Time

Had something happened
while I was asleep?
Sludge was standing by the door.
He would have barked or growled
if anyone had tried to come in.

I stared at the cage.
The cover looked
the same as before.
I peered inside.
There was a door,
and it was closed.

There were perches,
and they looked clean.
Everything looked clean.
Whoever had taken Hoot
had been careful to leave everything neat.
But who had taken her?
And how?
I needed time to think.
I needed pancakes.
"Wait here, Sludge," I said.

I rushed to the dining car.
I sat down.
A waiter came over.
"Has anyone ordered
a mouse to go?" I asked.
The waiter laughed. "A mouse?"
"Did you know there's
an owl on this train?" I asked.
The waiter shrugged.
"I heard people talking about it.
But nobody seems to have seen it."
I, Nate the Great,
was getting nowhere.
"May I have some pancakes
and one bone, please?"
"We have pancakes
with a wonderful fruit syrup,"
the waiter said.
"Fine," I said.

The food came fast.
I stared down at it.
The bone looked normal.
But my plate was dripping with syrup.
"Doesn't that look wonderful!"
the waiter said.
"No," I said. "It looks like a swamp
made of syrup."
The waiter smiled.
"This is a *blanket* of syrup.
The pancakes are tucked in under it."
"Tucked in? The pancakes are asleep?
Never mind. I'm hungry."

I ate and thought.
Did I have any clues?
Yes.
My biggest clue was that Sludge
is a great detective.
He had kept wagging his tail
as if nothing had happened.
As if no one had come into the room.
And I had other clues.
I finished my pancakes,

put the bone in my pocket,
and walked back to my room.
I opened the door.
Sludge wagged his tail.
I gave him the bone.
"We have solved the case," I said.
I picked up the owl cage.
"This cage is clean.
No stray feathers.
No bits or pieces of anything.
This is a new cage.
Never used.
Also, a waiter told me
that nobody seems to have seen the owl.
I, Nate the Great, say that
that nobody includes *us*!
You and I never saw Hoot
in this cage.
Because she was never in it!"

CHAPTER EIGHT

Sidetrack

Sludge looked puzzled.
"You're right," I said.
"We have not solved the case.
We still don't know
who wrote the note.
And we don't know why Olivia
wanted us to guard an empty cage.
She planned this well.
She didn't want me
to look in the cage.
That's why I was told that Hoot
needed a good day's sleep.

She told me about the mice
to make sure I wouldn't
try to feed Hoot.
And now, here we are,
you, me, and an empty cage
on a train
on the way to Los Angeles.
Olivia said she would catch
up with us. How could she
be sure of that?"
I, Nate the Great,
knew the answer.
Sludge and I stretched out
on a couch.

Good detectives know
when to take action
and when to wait.
This was a time to wait.
We waited. And waited.
At last a piece of paper
was slipped under our door.
I picked it up.
There was a message on it.

Olivia Sharp here.
In the private
car at the end of
the train.
Since you are a
great detective
you have figured
out:
(A) I have been on
this train all the
time.
(B) You are a body-
guard for a decoy.

"Come on, Sludge," I said.
Sludge and I walked to the last car.
I knocked on the door.
"Come in," Olivia called.
Sludge and I walked in.
Olivia was sitting behind a huge desk
with a computer, a telephone,
and piles of paper.

"I'm at work," she said.
"I'm writing up reports
on my last five cases."
"Where is Hoot?" I asked.
"Hidden on the train," Olivia said.
"Why didn't you tell me
the cage was empty?" I asked.
Olivia tossed her boa.
"Because I knew that
you and Sludge
would not want to guard
something that was nothing."
"Good thinking."
Olivia stood up. "So, did you
find out who wrote the note?"
"Yes. But Sludge and I must leave.
We will be back soon."

The Great Train Detective

Sludge and I were back
in ten minutes with
the lady with very clean feet,
the musician, and the Owl Man.
"Everybody please sit down," I said.
I turned to the lady.
"Hoot makes you sneeze.

But you sneezed when
I was with you
and Hoot wasn't.
So other things must
make you sneeze too."
"Yes," she said. "Turnips, glue,
petunias, dirty feet, cats,
chewing gum, anything pink,
fresh air, and spiders."
"Hmmm. So if Hoot wasn't around,
you would still sneeze."
"Yes."

"Then maybe you do like Hoot?"

"Nice owl. Good manners."

I turned to the musician.

"You like Hoot, correct?"

"Yes," said the musician.

I turned to the Owl Man.

"You do look like an owl," I said.

"But that's because you want to.

You wear spotted shirts,

you comb your hair into two points,

and you wear big yellow glasses.

You like looking like Hoot.

I, Nate the Great, say
that none of you
have a reason for
writing a terrible note about Hoot."
Then I turned to the musician.
"YOU wrote the note!"
"What?" The musician stood up.
"I did not write a terrible note.
I like owls."

"I believe you," I said.
Olivia walked up to me.
"Did you solve this case
or not?" she asked.
"Yes. I, Nate the Great, say that
the note was a get-well note!"
Olivia pulled the note
out of her pocket.
"It says that it will
be a happy day when Hoot
the owl flies *away*.
How can that be a get-well note?"
I turned to the musician again.
"You have a little trouble
writing rhymes, right?"
"Yes, and I needed something
to rhyme with *day*.
It was a good, friendly note."

"I, Nate the Great, say
that things that look good
to somebody
can look terrible
to somebody else.
Today I was served
food that looked good
to the waiter
and bad to me."
I turned to Olivia.
"End of case.
Hoot is safe."
Olivia tossed her boa
into the air.
"You were fabulous!"
she said.

"No," I said.

"Actually I was only great."

The boa landed on Sludge.

"I'll give you anything you want,"

Olivia said. "Make a list."

I reached into my pocket.

"Sludge and I came prepared," I said.

I handed Olivia a piece of paper.

WANT
25 bones
25 pancakes
without
syrup

DO NOT WANT
Cage, with
or without
owl
Boa, tossed
or otherwise

"Now tell me *exactly* where Hoot is,"

I said.

"She's still on the train," Olivia said.

Suddenly I, Nate the Great, knew Olivia

had given me a clue I did not want.

Sludge and I went back to our room
and sat by the window.
We were not alone.

~Extra~
Fun Activities!

What's Inside

Owls are strange. Trains are interesting. Nate wanted to know more about them. He snooped around the library. It is a good place for uncovering facts.

NATE'S NOTES: Owls

Owls live all over the world. They live in forests, grasslands, and deserts. The snowy owl lives in the Arctic!

Owls see better than dogs. They see much better than humans. An owl can see a mouse in a field a mile away.

Owls can turn their heads three-quarters of the way around. That's more than twice as far as people can turn their heads.

Snowy Owl

Screech Owl

Great Horned Owl

Owls' eyes don't move. Humans can move their eyes up, down, left, right, and around in a circle.

An owl's eyes are huge. They take up about half of the owl's skull. That doesn't leave much room for the owl's brain.

Some stories say owls are wise. Are they? Probably not. But owls are good hunters. They can fly without making a sound.

Owls fly very quietly. Their thick, soft feathers absorb the sound of their huge wings fanning the air. Owls can move their wings very slowly. That cuts down on noise, too.

Barn Owl

Burrowing Owl

Barred Owl

Owls usually sleep during the day. They wake up and hunt at night. They eat mice, insects, and small birds. They also eat fish and snakes and other reptiles.

Owls swallow their food whole. They spit out pellets of fur and tiny bones. Their stomachs can't handle that stuff.

Owls can see during the day. They close their eyes halfway to block out bright light. That makes them look sleepy even when they're wide awake.

Owls have excellent hearing. They can hear tiny mouse steps.

An owl has eight talons. These are sharp claws. They help the owl hold on to a branch while sleeping. The owl also uses its talons to tear food apart.

An owl can eat as many as six mice in one day.

Nate's Notes: Trains

The steepest train track in the world is in Switzerland. It goes to the top of Pilatus Mountain. It first ran in 1889.

The highest train track is in Peru. It was built more than a hundred years ago. It has fifty-nine bridges and sixty-six tunnels. The railway climbs to 15,685 feet above sea level. Many people get sick from traveling so high. There is a doctor on board to treat them.

The longest straight stretch of train track is in Australia. It goes more than three hundred miles without taking a turn.

The fastest train is the TGV. It runs in France. It once went 322 miles per hour.

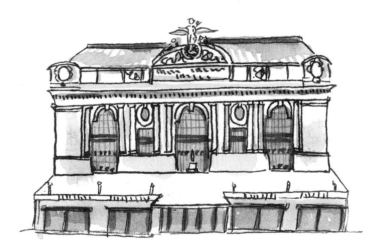

The largest train station is in New York City. It is called Grand Central Terminal. It has forty-four train platforms.

The Orient Express is a famous old
train. It traveled from Paris to
Bucharest. It crossed through six
countries. Sometimes kings and
queens traveled on it.

The longest train route is the one
taken by the Trans-Siberian Express. It
travels 5,778 miles. The trip takes nine
days. It makes ninety-one stops.

Many railroads have cool bridges. The Kinzua Bridge in Pennsylvania was once the highest railroad bridge in the world. It was built in 1882. It is about thirty stories tall. A tornado damaged the bridge in 2003.

One of the tallest railroad bridges in Europe is in Montenegro. It is 650 feet high.

Nate guarded Hoot.
Other people guard
more important things.
Here's more of what Nate
uncovered at the library.

NATE'S NOTES: Guarding Things

The Household Troops guard the
Queen of England. She lives in
Buckingham Palace in London. The
guards wear red uniforms. They
have tall fur hats. The hats are
called bearskins.

Visitors sometimes try to make the
guards smile. It's almost impossible!

When a new group of guards
starts work every day, there's a
ceremony called the Changing
of the Guard. It takes forty-
five minutes.

Fort Knox is in Kentucky. Inside is more than six billion dollars' worth of gold! The gold is in the form of small bricks. The gold bricks are called bullion.

The gold belongs to the U.S. government. It's kept in a secure room called a vault. The vault door weighs twenty tons. It's as heavy as three elephants!

There's a lock on the door. It takes several people to open the lock. Each person enters a few numbers of the combination.

No visitors are allowed inside. U.S. soldiers guard Fort Knox.

The most valuable thing in ancient Egypt was the king's body—after he died! Why? Ancient Egyptians believed a dead king could come back to life. When that happened, the king would need his stuff. They buried him with food, drink, and clothing. The king would also need his body. The Egyptians worked very hard to protect the king's body.

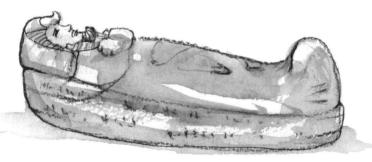

They built huge tombs for their kings. The biggest of all is the pyramid of Khufu. A pyramid is a giant stone building. The king is buried deep inside, in a tiny chamber.

Kings were buried with gold and jewels. Many people wanted to steal from the tombs. That's why the door of Khufu's pyramid is hidden. It looks like solid stone. The builders also made traps to catch thieves. Fake stones covered deep holes. Trapdoors snapped shut and held thieves inside.

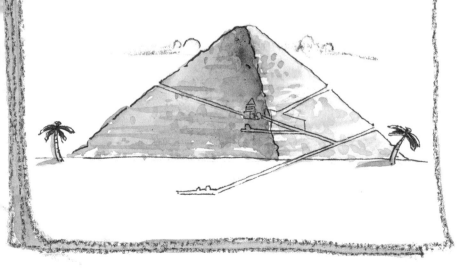

The Owl Express Quiz

1. Who can see best?
   a. Nate
   b. Hoot
   c. Olivia Sharp
   d. Fang

2. What are owls good at?
   a. hunting
   b. flying quietly
   c. giving wise advice
   d. both a and b

3. What is an owl pellet?
   a. owl poop
   b. something the owl coughs up
   c. dried owl food
   d. a place where pet owls sleep

4. Where is the longest stretch of straight railroad track?
   a. in Peru
   b. in the Grand Canyon
   c. in Australia
   d. in California

5. Where is the largest train station?
   a. in London
   b. in Paris
   c. in New York City
   d. in Montenegro

Train and Owl Riddles

What's the difference between a teacher and a train?
A teacher tells you to spit out your gum. A train says "chew chew!"

What happened when the T. rex took the train home?
He had to bring it back!

What happened when the owl lost his voice?
He didn't give a hoot!

Why did the owl howl?
Because the woodpecker pecked her.

Knock knock.
Who's there?
Owl.
Owl who?
Owl aboard!

How do you know owls are wiser than chickens?
Have you ever heard of Kentucky Fried Owl?

Where does a 500-pound owl sit?
Wherever it wants!

What does a 500-pound owl say?
"Here, kitty, kitty."

Chocolate Nests Recipe

Owls live in nests. People eat chocolate nests.

Ask an adult to help with this recipe. It will make about eight nests.

GET TOGETHER:

- one 14-ounce can of sweetened condensed milk
- one 12-ounce bag of chocolate chips
- one 5-ounce can of chow mein noodles
- a cup of jelly beans
- a mixing bowl
- a potholder
- a cookie sheet
- waxed paper
- spoons

HOW TO MAKE YOUR CHOCOLATE NESTS:

1. Pour the condensed milk into the bowl. Add the chocolate chips. Microwave at low power until the chips melt.
2. Using the potholder, remove the bowl from the microwave. Be careful!
3. Pour the noodles into the bowl. Mix them with the chocolate.
4. Cover the cookie sheet with waxed paper. Drop a couple of spoonfuls of the chocolate mixture onto the paper. Press the mixture into the shape of a nest.
5. Add a few jelly beans. These are your eggs.
6. Chill the nests for several hours.
7. Eat!

How to Make a Pinecone Owl

This owl is a good pet. You don't need to feed him.
He'll never need a bodyguard.

GET TOGETHER:

- a black marker
- white construction paper
- safety scissors
- two acorns
- white glue
- one fat pinecone
- yellow construction paper
- a small branch

HOW TO MAKE YOUR PINECONE OWL:

1. Make your owl's eyes: Draw two dime-sized circles on the white paper. Cut them out. Color black circles in the center of each one.
2. Remove the caps from the acorns. Glue the paper eyes inside the caps. Glue the caps to the pinecone.
3. Make your owl's beak: Cut a triangle from the yellow paper. Glue it onto the pinecone.
4. Give your owl a place to sit: Glue the pinecone onto the branch.

How to Make a Twinkie Train

Riding trains is fun. Eating trains is fun, too.

GET TOGETHER:

- a Twinkie
- tubes of frosting in different colors
- whipped cream cheese
- six vanilla wafers
- a marshmallow

HOW TO MAKE YOUR TWINKIE TRAIN:

1. Unwrap the Twinkie. Use frosting to make it look like a train. Try drawing windows and doors.
2. Use cream cheese to glue on vanilla wafers for wheels.
3. The marshmallow is your smokestack. Glue it on with the cream cheese.
4. Make a frosting track on a plate. Take your train for a ride.
5. Eat!

Train Talking

Trains have a language of their own.
Learn how to talk like a conductor.

A **caboose** is a car attached to the end of the train.
The people working on the train use the caboose as
an office on wheels.

A **conductor** is the worker in charge of the train.
She collects tickets, too.

A **cowcatcher** is an iron wedge mounted on the front
of an engine. It works like a plow. It clears the tracks
of tree branches, snow, and even cows!

The **crew** is all the people who work on a train.

The **engineer** runs the locomotive. (More about
locomotives on the next page.)

Freight is the cargo, or stuff, that trains carry. People
are not freight. They are passengers.

A **grease monkey** is the worker who keeps the train well oiled.

Kingpin is another name for the conductor.

A **locomotive** is the train car with the engine inside. It pushes or pulls the other cars.

The **main line** is the most important route on a railroad. Smaller routes are called branch lines.

If a train crew **puts it on the ground,** that means they've crashed the train!

Trains run on **rails**. These are a pair of metal bars attached to the ground.

A fast freight train is a **red ball**.

A **roundhouse** is a round building where workers clean and repair trains.

A **terminal** is a place where passengers wait for their trains. Freight is loaded and unloaded there.

A **station** is a place where the train stops.

A word about learning with

Nate the Great

The Nate the Great series is good fun and has been entertaining children for over forty years. These books are also valuable learning tools in and out of the classroom.

Nate's world—his home, his friends, his neighborhood—is one that every young person recognizes. Nate introduces beginning readers and those who have graduated to early chapter books to the detective mystery genre, and they respond to Nate's commitment to solving the case and helping his friends.

What's more, as Nate the Great solves his cases, readers learn with him. Nate unravels mysteries by using evidence collection, cogent reasoning, problem-solving, analytical skills, and logic in a way that teaches readers to develop critical-thinking abilities. The stories help children start discussions about how to approach difficult situations and give them tools to resolve them.

When you read a Nate the Great book with a child, or when a child reads a Nate the Great mystery on his or her own, the child is guaranteed a satisfying ending that will have taught him or her important classroom and life skills. We know that you and your children will enjoy reading and learning from Nate the Great's wonderful stories as much as we do.

Find out more at NatetheGreat.com.

Happy reading and learning with Nate!

Solve all the mysteries with

Nate the Great

MARJORIE WEINMAN SHARMAT has written more than 130 books for children and young adults, as well as movie and TV novelizations. Her books have been translated into twenty-four languages. The award-winning Nate the Great series, hailed in *Booklist* as "groundbreaking," was inspired by her father, Nathan Weinman. Marjorie Weinman Sharmat and her husband, Mitchell Sharmat, have written many books together, including the Olivia Sharp series, based on his concept of detective Olivia Sharp, Agent for Secrets.

MITCHELL SHARMAT, a graduate of Harvard University, has written numerous picture books, easy readers, and novels, and is a contributor to many textbook reading programs. He is best known for the classic *Gregory, the Terrible Eater*, a *Reading Rainbow* Feature Selection and a *New York Times* Critics' Pick. In Mitchell Sharmat's honor, The Sharmat Collection, displaying the books he's written, was established at the Harvard Graduate School of Education by the Munroe C. Gutman Library.

MARTHA WESTON illustrated *How Will the Easter Bunny Know?* by Kay Winters (Yearling), as well as more than forty books for children, including six she also wrote.